CW01220075

Ganesha

The Elephant-Headed God

Wonder House

Printed 2019

Wonder House
(An imprint of Prakash Books Pvt. Ltd.)

Wonder House Books
Corporate & Editorial Office
113-A, 1st Floor, Ansari Road,
Daryaganj, New Delhi-110002
Tel +91 11 2324 7062-65

© Wonder House 2019

All rights reserved. No part of this book may be reproduced or transmitted in any form by any means, electronic or mechanical, including photocopying and recording, or by any information storage and retrieval system except as may be expressly permitted in writing by the publisher.

ISBN : 978-93-89432-41-1

Printed in India

Contents

Nandi and the Door 4

Heramba 10

Shiva Retaliates 14

Revenge for Kartikeya 20

The Elephant Head 26

Kuber's Feast 32

A Lesson for Kuber 36

Sage Agastya's Kamandalu 48

Ganesha Creates a River 52

Ganesha and the Cat 56

A Toothsome Tale 60

Ganesha's Journey Around the World 66

The Return of Kartikeya 72

Ganesha Becomes a Writer 74

Chapter 1
Nandi and the Door

The magnificent Mount Kailash was Lord Shiva and Goddess Parvati's abode. One day, Goddess Parvati summoned Nandi, the guardian of Kailash. Soon, Nandi stood before her. "Mother, command me, how can I serve you?" Nandi bowed down.

Parvati said, "Nandi, today I don't want to be troubled, so guard the door and let no one inside."

She then went to take a bath. Nandi stood guard at the palace entrance and intended to faithfully carry out Parvati's wishes.

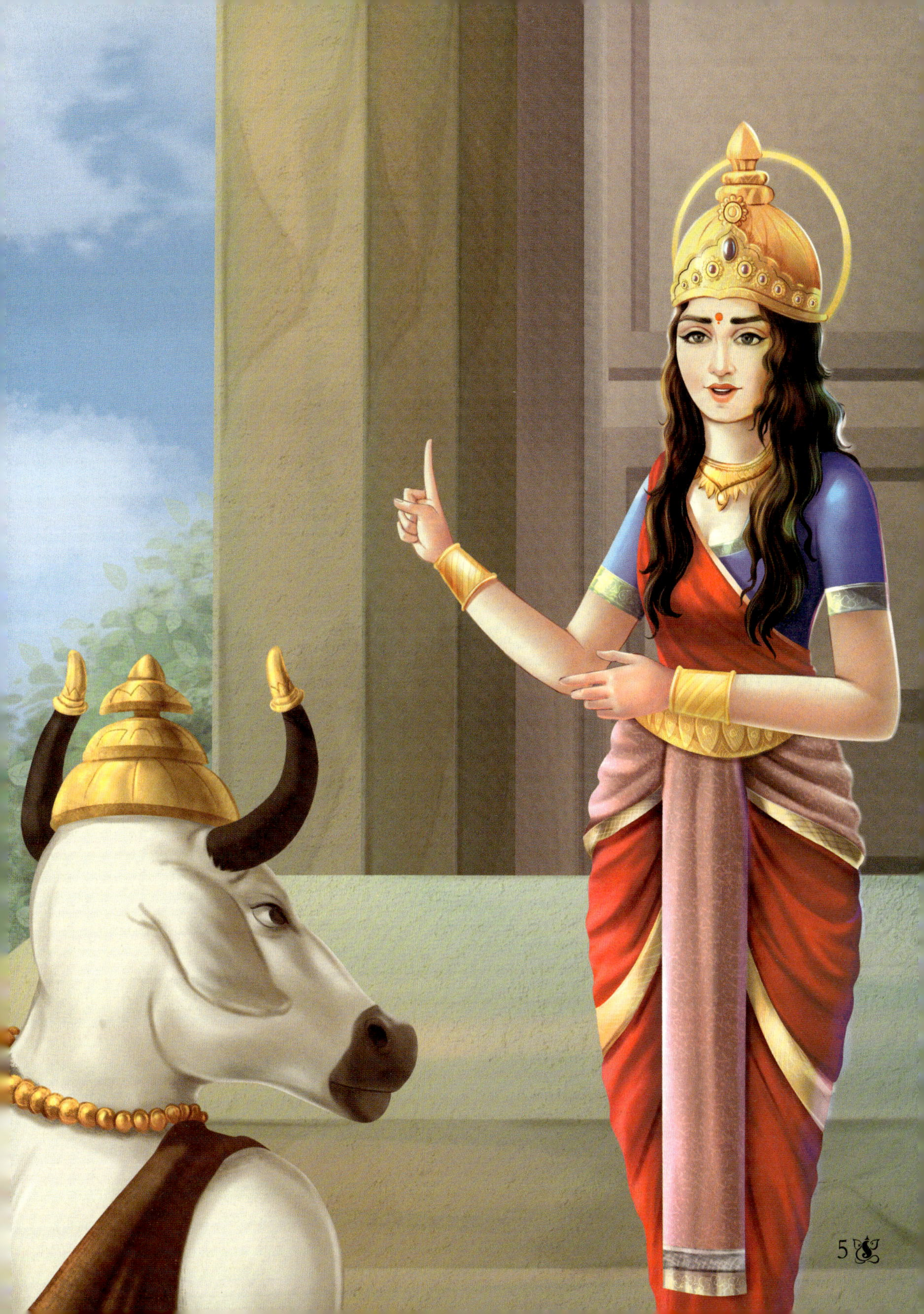

Ganesha The Elephant-Headed God

Lord Shiva's arrival put Nadni in a grave dilemma.

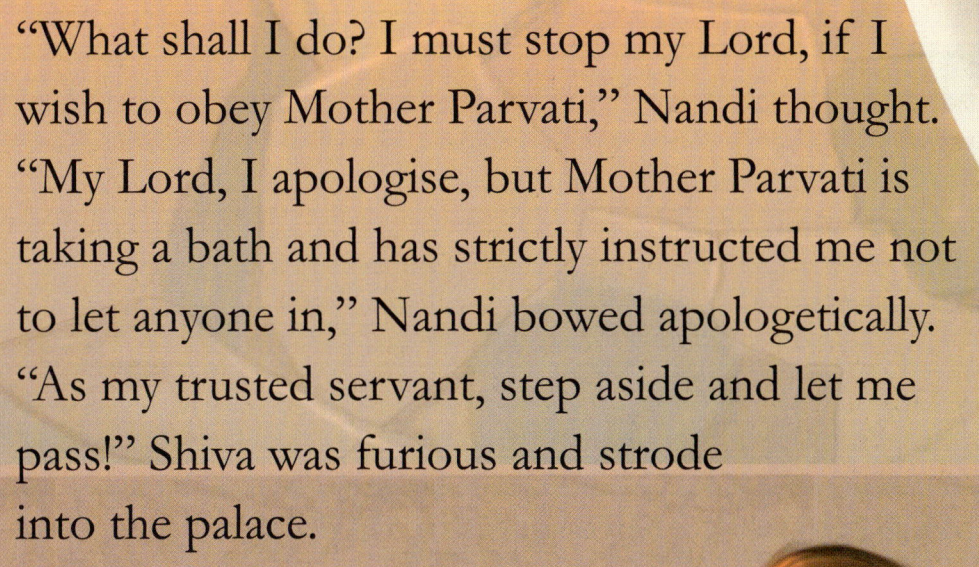

"What shall I do? I must stop my Lord, if I wish to obey Mother Parvati," Nandi thought. "My Lord, I apologise, but Mother Parvati is taking a bath and has strictly instructed me not to let anyone in," Nandi bowed apologetically. "As my trusted servant, step aside and let me pass!" Shiva was furious and strode into the palace.

"Mahadev, what brings you here?" Parvati was angry at this intrusion of her privacy. Shiva was amused and tried to soothe her.

Ganesha The Elephant-Headed God

However, Parvati was upset that she had no one as loyal as Nandi was to Shiva. She approached Nandi at the palace gates.

"I commanded you to guard the door and not let anyone in without my permission! But you didn't obey me!" Parvati was enraged.

"Mother! My loyalty first lies with Shiva, I cannot revolt against him. He questioned my faith in him," Nandi replied. Parvati was disappointed and sent Nandi away. Parvati discussed the matter with her friends. One of them suggested, "Why don't you create an attendant of your own, one who shall be loyal only to you."

Chapter 2

Heramba

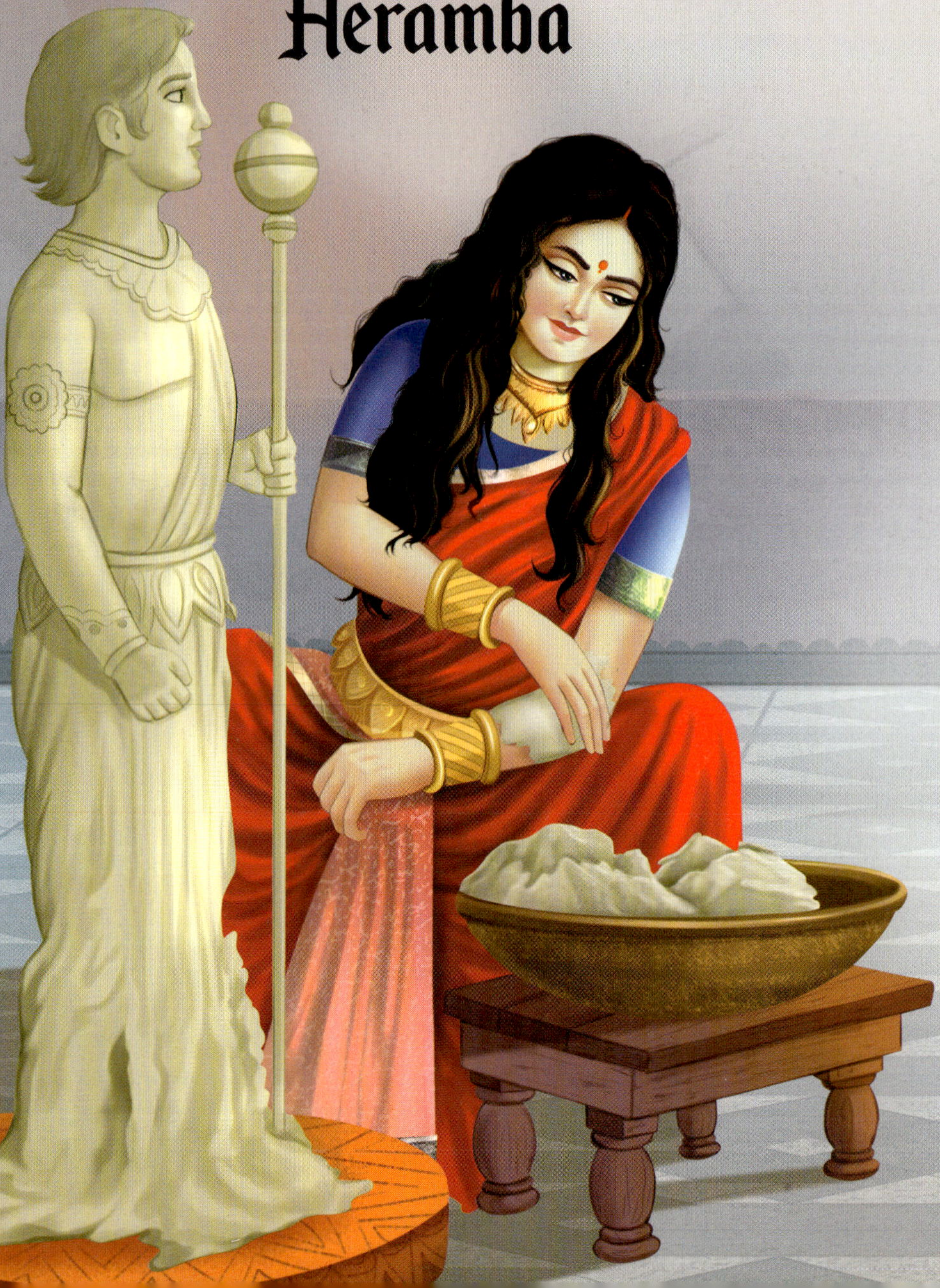

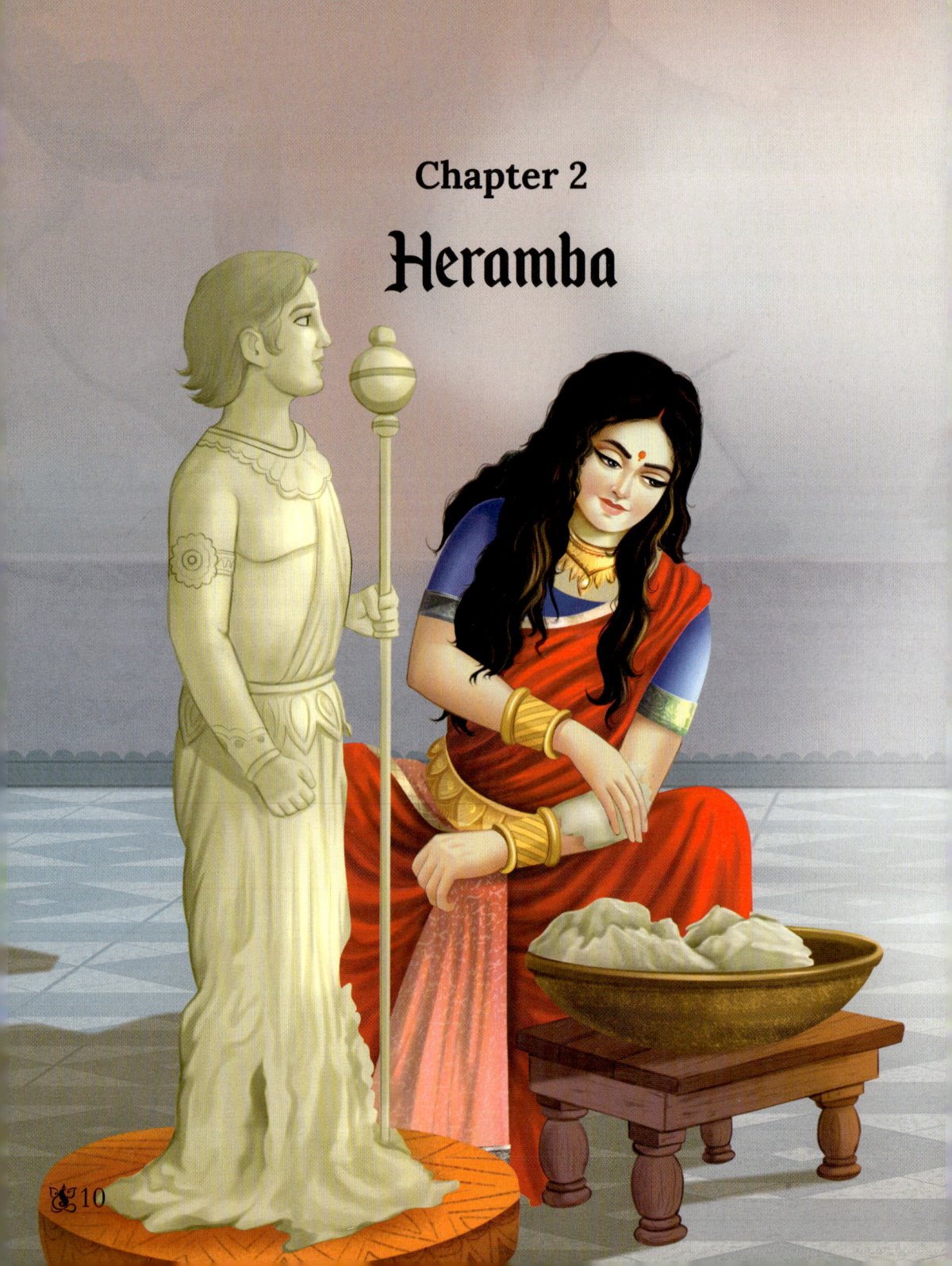

Parvati decided that it was a good idea. She went inside the palace chambers and collected some turmeric paste.

She gathered saffron from her body and made a statue of a child. Then she breathed life into it. Parvati was pleased with her own creation and blessed him.

"You are my loyal son, Heramba. My dear child, you must promise to guard the palace entrance and not let anyone in. Not even Mahadev!" said Parvati.

"I promise you, mother," said the child and accepted a staff as a weapon from Parvati.

Ganesha The Elephant-Headed God

Heramba patiently stood at the entrance. Shortly after, Lord Shiva returned. He failed to recognise the boy, and to his astonishment, the boy blocked his way. "Who are you? Move aside! Let me pass. I am Shiva, one of the creators of the universe," Shiva spoke with authority.

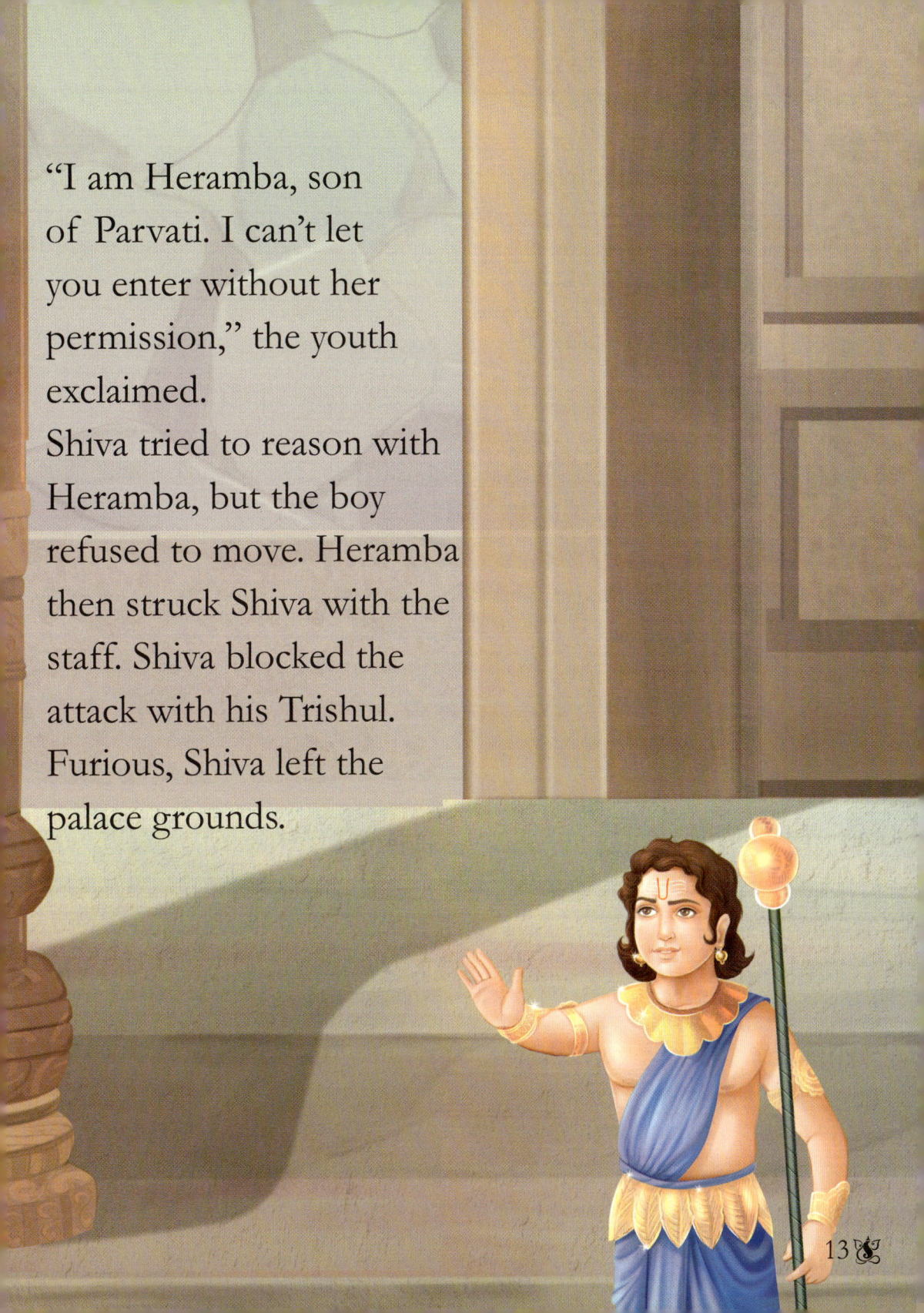

"I am Heramba, son of Parvati. I can't let you enter without her permission," the youth exclaimed.

Shiva tried to reason with Heramba, but the boy refused to move. Heramba then struck Shiva with the staff. Shiva blocked the attack with his Trishul. Furious, Shiva left the palace grounds.

Chapter 3
Shiva Retaliates

Shiva returned to Mount Kailash, where his attendants sensed his turmoil. "Mahadev, you look upset. What is bothering you?" Nandi asked.

"I went to my palace, but there was a foolish boy who wouldn't let me enter!" exclaimed Shiva.

"How can anyone dare to stop you?" Nandi said, astonished.

"Nandi, I order you to defeat this youth and take him as a prisoner," Shiva said sharply.

Nandi marched towards the palace to execute Shiva's command.

Ganesha The Elephant-Headed God

At the palace gates, Heramba stood resolutely holding his staff. He refused to move aside even when he saw Shiva's followers approaching him. "I warn you, boy! If you don't move aside, you'll face our wrath!" Nandi warned Heramba. "I will allow someone in only when Mother Parvati says so," said Heramba. "You foolish child, I challenge you to a duel," Nandi raised his staff.

They started fighting, but soon Heramba threw Nandi on the ground, and Lord Shiva's disciples were stunned at the boy's strength. They attacked him but were overpowered easily.

Defeated by the youth, Nandi and the other disciples fled the battlefield.

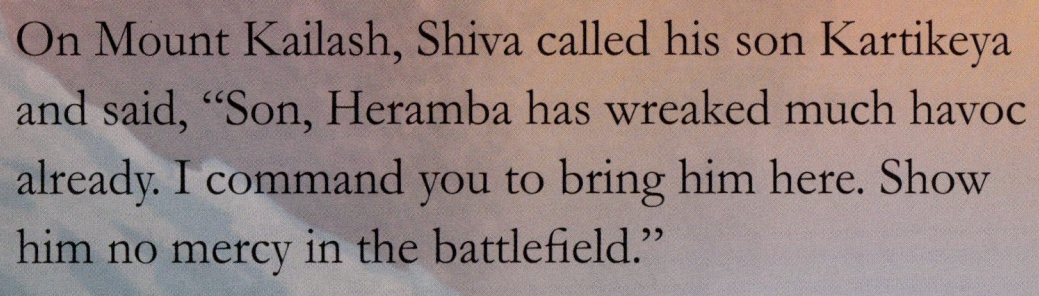

On Mount Kailash, Shiva called his son Kartikeya and said, "Son, Heramba has wreaked much havoc already. I command you to bring him here. Show him no mercy in the battlefield."

Kartikeya was sceptical about fighting his own brother. But he couldn't disobey his father and went ahead.

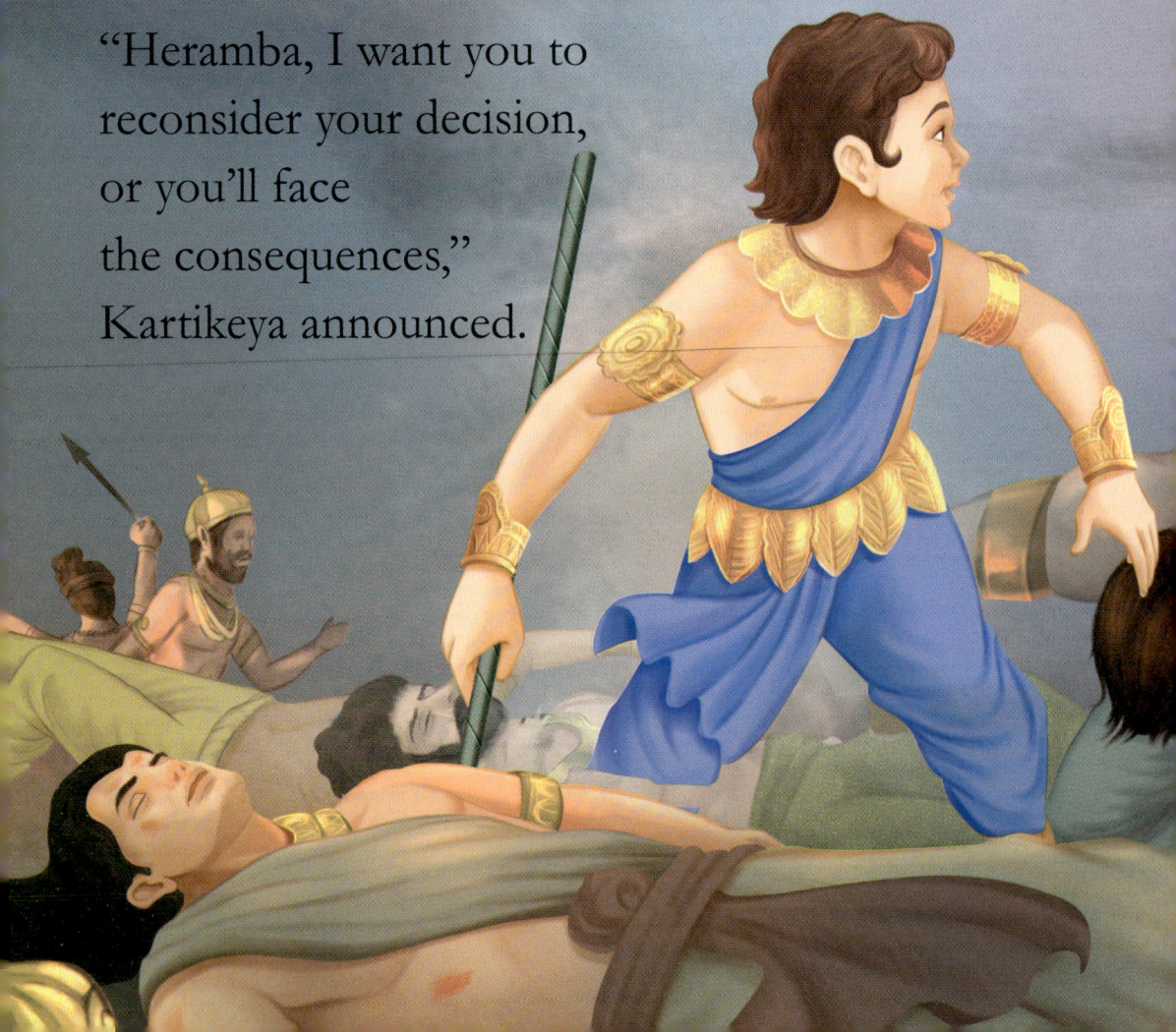

"Heramba, I want you to reconsider your decision, or you'll face the consequences," Kartikeya announced.

But Heramba refused to go back on his promise and the brothers started to fight. They both had similar combat skills, but, at last, Heramba attacked him with his staff. Kartikeya fainted immediately.

Chapter 4
Revenge for Kartikeya

Nandi returned to Shiva carrying an unconscious Kartikeya in his hands. Seeing his son's condition aggravated Shiva and he said, "I'll kill that youth with my bare hands."

Lord Vishnu came forward and said, "Mahadev, suppress your anger. Let me settle this without further bloodshed."

But Shiva had run out of patience, so, with his army of Ganas and other Devas, he advanced to the palace.

Sensing danger to Heramba's life, Parvati summoned Goddesses Kali and Durga to protect her son.

They gave all their strength to Heramba. Heramba was unfazed by Shiva and defeated his huge army. Shiva fired the most potent weapons at Heramba, but none of them killed him.

Ganesha The Elephant-Headed God

Lord Vishnu wanted to end the battle between Shiva and Heramba. So he decided to intervene and said, "Mahadev, let me handle the youth with my supreme power."

Vishnu charged at Heramba. When that didn't work, he mounted his vehicle, Garuda, and attacked him from the sky, but Heramba stood strong.

Lord Vishnu broke Heramba's staff in two, and to Vishnu's utter shock, the youth started fighting with his bare hands. So far a spectator, Lord Shiva realised that Heramba was dominating the fight.

Ganesha The Elephant-Headed God

So, Shiva hurled his Trishul at him to end the fight immediately. The Trishul was Shiva's most powerful weapon and it severed Heramba's head. Shiva had killed Parvati's son Heramba.

Vishnu was aghast and said, "How will we ever pacify Mother Parvati? Her anger and retribution will be catastrophic!"

Parvati was in the bath when she heard the news of her son's death. She was filled with grief and wept bitterly. But, soon, her sorrow turned into a fury that knew no bounds and threatened to destroy the world.

Ganesha The Elephant-Headed God

Chapter 5
The Elephant Head

She decided to destroy the entire universe as a consequence of the Devas' actions. Brahma witnessed the wrath of Parvati and apologised to her on behalf of Shiva. "Mother! Forgive us and please don't destroy the universe," pleaded Brahma.

"You all killed my son, who was simply following my orders," Parvati roared. Vishnu, Indra, and Brahma tried to put an end to the destruction and feared complete annihilation. But Parvati didn't stop and manifested hundreds of goddesses, who started wreaking havoc on the gods.

"I shall be calm only when my son is brought back to life," Parvati replied.

Ganesha The Elephant-Headed God

The gods went to Lord Shiva and appealed, "Lord, we are being punished by Mother Parvati, and we request you to resurrect Heramba."

"I accept your request and instruct you to go in the northern direction. Bring me the head of the first animal you come across," Shiva replied.

The gods followed the instruction and went to the forest. They returned with the head of an elephant. Shiva chanted the Mahamritunjaya mantra, placing the elephant head on Heramba's body. Heramba was alive once again.

Ganesha The Elephant-Headed God

When Parvati saw her son breathing, she rushed forward to embrace him.

"He has transformed into a humble person. He shall be eternally divine and be acknowledged as the god of knowledge and wisdom throughout the world.

He will be known as Ganesha, the head of the Ganas, and shall be worshipped first, before every auspicious event," Shiva declared.

Parvati was satisfied with Shiva's blessings. Shiva and Parvati went back to their abode along with their two sons. The gods worshipped Ganesha and returned to their respective abodes as well.

Chapter 6

Kuber's Feast

One day, Kuber, the god of wealth came to meet Lord Shiva and Parvati. Kuber believed that he was the richest god of all.

"What brings you here, Kuber?" Shiva asked politely. Kuber bowed down and said, "I am going to hold a lavish dinner at my place and have come here to invite you and Mother Parvati."

The divine couple knew that Kuber just wanted to show off his riches to them, so they declined his invitation.

"Ganesha is fond of eating, so take him with you," Shiva said warmly.

Ganesha The Elephant-Headed God

34

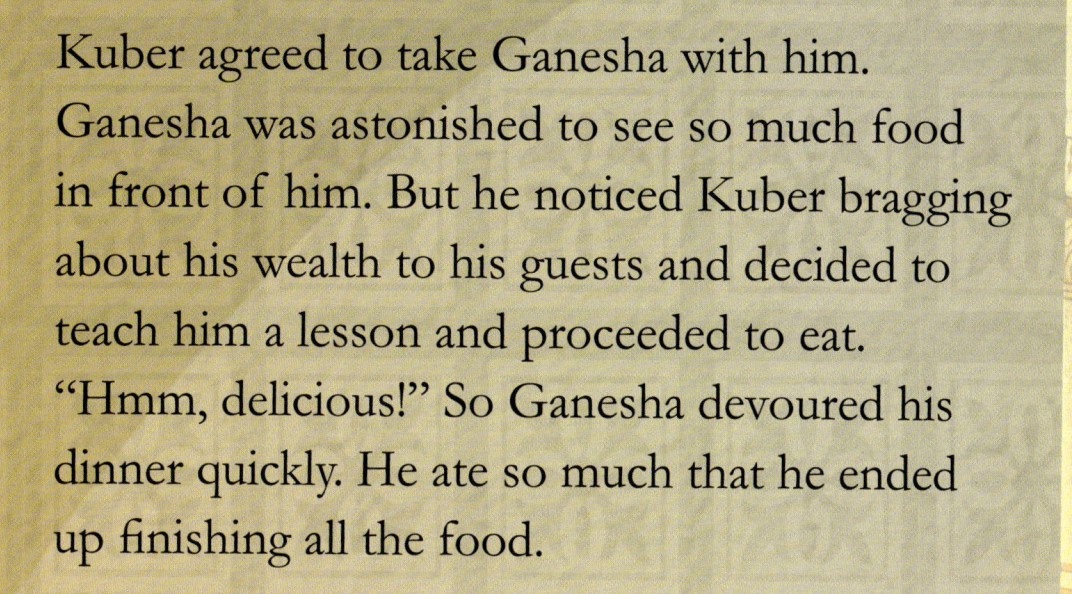

Kuber agreed to take Ganesha with him. Ganesha was astonished to see so much food in front of him. But he noticed Kuber bragging about his wealth to his guests and decided to teach him a lesson and proceeded to eat. "Hmm, delicious!" So Ganesha devoured his dinner quickly. He ate so much that he ended up finishing all the food.

Ganesha The Elephant-Headed God

Chapter 7
A Lesson for Kuber

Ganesha didn't stop eating and ate all the food cooked for the feast. There was hardly any food left for the other guests. So he moved on to Kuber's wealth and started to eat all the gold. Then he began to eat vessels, dishes, furniture, and other things in Kuber's city. The guests were amazed at Ganesha's feat.

Ganesha's hunger was still not satisfied, and he demanded more food. Kuber was embarrassed in front of his guests.

Ganesha The Elephant-Headed God

Ganesha went to the kitchen and ate all the food stored there. The servants came out running from the kitchen and complained to Kuber, "Lord, Ganesha gobbled everything, there is nothing left to serve to the other guests." Kuber was terrified. He cautiously approached Ganesha and lamented, "I apologise Ganesha, but there isn't a single grain I can offer you now."

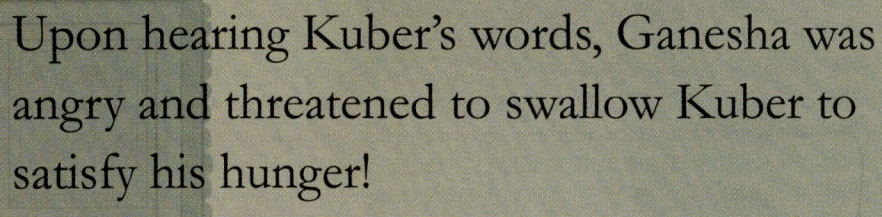

Upon hearing Kuber's words, Ganesha was angry and threatened to swallow Kuber to satisfy his hunger!

Kuber panicked and rushed to Lord Shiva's abode, Mount Kailash, for protection.

Ganesha The Elephant-Headed God

"Mahadev, save me and tell me a way to satisfy Ganesha's hunger," he begged Shiva and Parvati.

Shiva gave him a bowl of cereal and said, "Serve this to Ganesha with humility."

Kuber realised his mistake and asked for forgiveness for his pride and learnt a lesson in humility.

He offered the bowl to Ganesha. Ganesha's hunger was quenched after eating the cereal.

Ganesha The Elephant-Headed God

After Ganesha stuffed himself at Kuber's house, he proceeded to leave. He ate so much that he got a pot-belly and it became difficult for him to even walk.

He then called his vehicle, Mooshak, which was a mouse, and mounted it.

But Ganesha was so heavy that his vehicle also got tired. Suddenly, he fell off his vehicle.

"Why did you drop me?" Ganesha asked his mouse. The mouse feared punishment and pointed towards a snake at a distance.

Ganesha The Elephant-Headed God

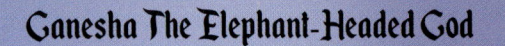

"Lord, it wasn't my fault, this snake came in my way," said the mouse.
The moon had been watching the entire scene unfold and began to laugh at Ganesha's predicament. Ganesha picked up the snake and threw it as far as he could.

Then he turned to the moon and said, "You made fun of me and humiliated me!"
The moon continued laughing, which made Ganesha furious. Ganesha cursed the moon, making it completely invisible.

Ganesha The Elephant-Headed God

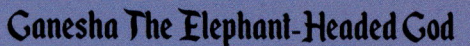

"Forgive me, Lord! I didn't mean to offend you. How will I live without my shine? Please take your curse back," the moon begged Ganesha. "Laughing at somebody else's weaknesses or deformities doesn't suit you. It was impolite of you," Ganesha said.

The moon realised his mistake and asked for forgiveness. Ganesha saw a change in the moon's behaviour and said, "I'll forgive you! You'll appear and disappear every 15 days in a set cycle. That way, you will not lose your shine."

Ganesha The Elephant-Headed God

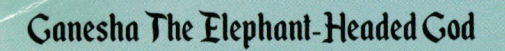

Chapter 8
Sage Agastya's Kamandalu

While on Mount Kailash, Sage Agastya sought the blessings of Lord Brahma and Lord Shiva. The sage wished to create a river in the southern lands. The gods fulfilled his wish and filled his Kamandalu with sacred water and said, "A river will flow wherever you pour the water of this Kamandalu. All the animals and villagers will rejoice and have their fill."

Agastya was pleased and headed to the mountains of Coorg. He was tired and began to look for a place where he could rest.

Ganesha The Elephant-Headed God

Sage Agastya came across a small boy standing behind a tree.

"Who's standing there? Come out," he asked curiously.

The boy was Ganesha himself, and he told the sage that he was just playing with his vehicle, the mouse. Ganesha was curious about the sage's Kamandalu and asked about its purpose. The sage told Ganesha what he had planned.

"Ganesha, I walked all day, and now my legs hurt very much. I request you to hold this Kamandalu till I rest. But make sure that not a single drop spills from it," Agastya said.

Ganesha The Elephant-Headed God

Chapter 9
Ganesha Creates a River

Ganesha assured Agastya that he would guard the Kamandalu. Then Agastya sat on a hill-top to get some peace.

"Everyone here in the mountains of Coorg is thirsty and crying for water. Without water, the plants are withering, and the animals are starting to die. We should not cause any more delay, but Sage Agastya looks very tired," Ganesha said to his mouse.

He realised that it was an ideal location for the river. Ganesha set the Kamandalu down and took the form of a crow.

Ganesha The Elephant-Headed God

When Sage Agastya came back, he saw a crow hovering over the Kamandalu. Then it landed on the pot. Agastya tried to shoo off the bird. But the crow flew off flapping its wings and tipped the pot to the ground.
"What has this crow done!" Agastya was appalled.

Water started to flow out of the Kamandalu. First, it began as a trickle, then a stream, and as it flowed down the hills, it took the form of a river. It was later named Kaveri.

"Sage Agastya, I apologise that it didn't work out the way you had wished. Nevertheless, you have blessed this dried land," Ganesha bowed and left.

Ganesha The Elephant-Headed God

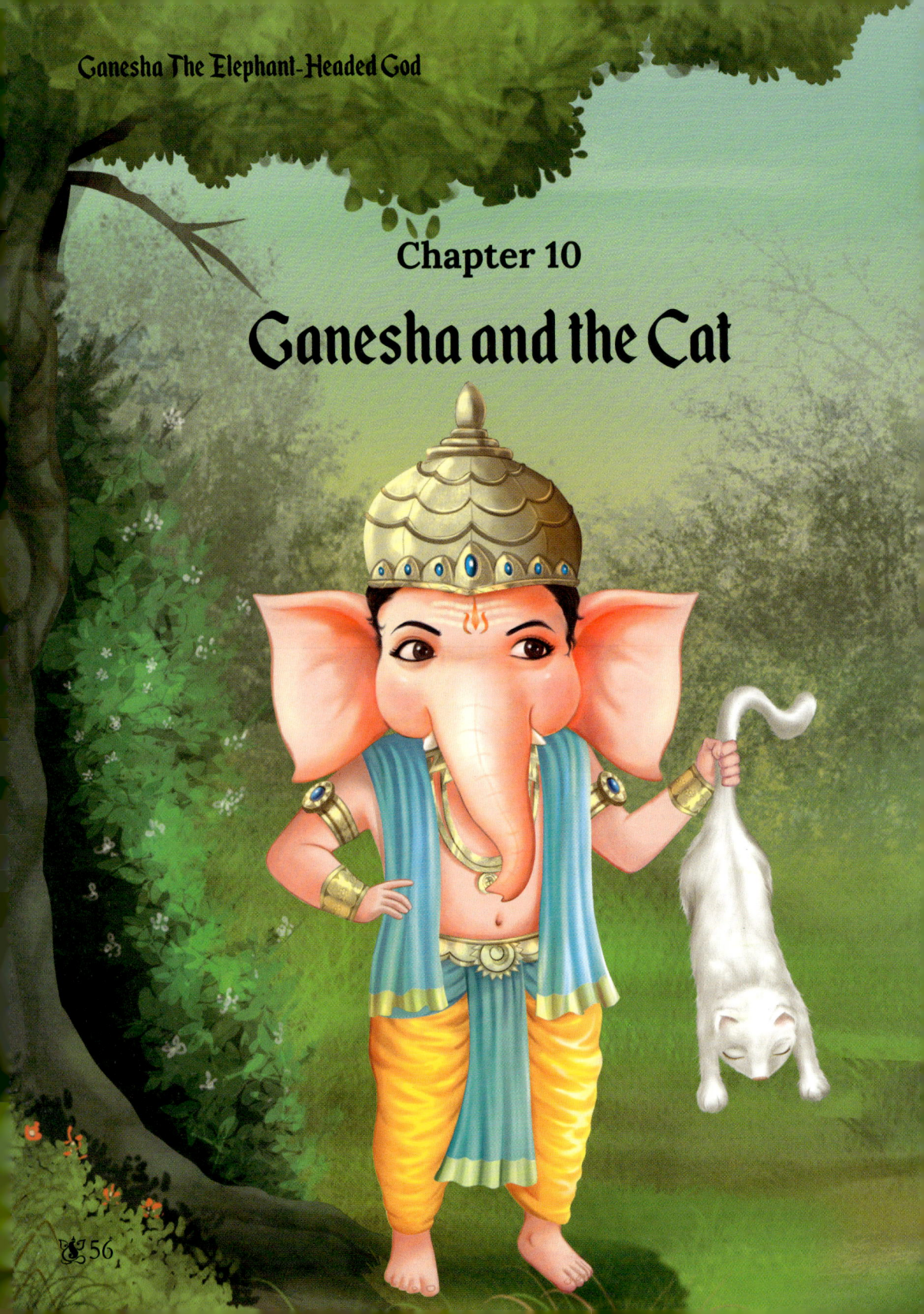

Chapter 10

Ganesha and the Cat

Ganesha was a mischievous child and often harassed defenceless animals. One day, he went out to play with his friends and his vehicle, Mooshak. Suddenly, Ganesha came across a white cat coming out of the bushes.
"O look! This cat also came to play with us!" Ganesha said laughing. Ganesha and his friends surrounded the cat and proceeded to tease it. He troubled and mistreated it for a long time. He then pulled its tail, but the cat meowed in pain. Having played the whole day, Ganesha was tired, so he let the cat go away.

Ganesha The Elephant-Headed God

Ganesha went back to Mount Kailash.
But, there he was shocked to see his lovely
Mother Parvati in a wounded condition.
Her face and arms were all scratched.
"Who did this to you, Mother?" Ganesha
asked worriedly.
"You, my child! I wanted to play with
my son, so I disguised myself as a cat,"
Parvati said. She then told her son that the
mistreatment of animals reflected
poorly on his own mother.
Ganesha repented his actions.
He promised to treat animals
gently, and treated them
with love and affection.

Ganesha The Elephant-Headed God

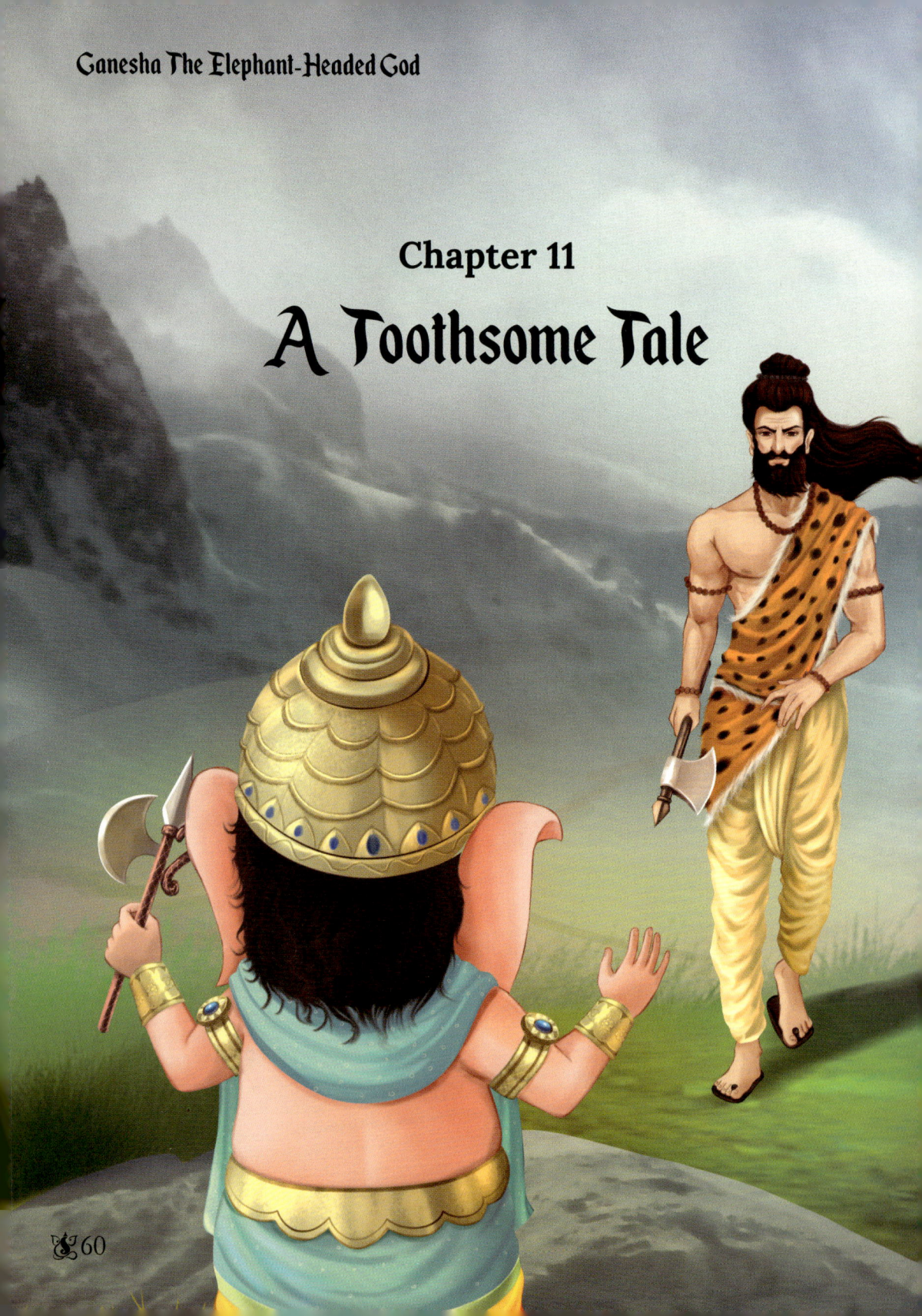

Chapter 11
A Toothsome Tale

Parashurama was known to be the axe-wielding incarnation of Vishnu. In the past, Lord Shiva had granted him a boon of immense power to defeat his enemies. Parashurama had successfully destroyed an entire demon army, and the kings who allied with them. After the war ended, Parashurama went to Mount Kailash to thank and pay his gratitude to Lord Shiva. But Ganesha stopped him at the entrance of Mount Kailash.

"I have come to meet Lord Shiva, let me enter his abode," Parashurama politely asked him to clear the way. But Ganesha didn't budge from his stance.

Ganesha The Elephant-Headed God

"Parashurama Ji, Mahadev wouldn't like it if someone disturbed him during meditation," Ganesha said.
"You haven't seen my anger! There's no one in this world who can stop me. Move!" Parashurama commenced walking, but Ganesha again denied him entry.

Parashurama was enraged, and a battle ensued with Ganesha. For a while, Ganesha seemed to be winning. Then, Parashurama took out the divine axe, Parashu, which he had received from Shiva.

It was the same axe that had helped him fight all the corrupt demons.

An angry Parashurama didn't think much and attacked poor Ganesha with his axe.

Ganesha The Elephant-Headed God

Ganesha noticed it coming his way, but this time, he didn't move.

"I can't disrespect the Parashu that was gifted to you by my father," with this, Ganesha allowed Parashurama's weapon to hit him. It chopped off his left tusk.

Shiva and Parvati came out running and saw Ganesha on the ground, groaning in pain. Parashurama felt guilty for his actions and begged the divine couple to forgive him.

"Apologising won't bring my son's tooth back," Parvati blamed him.

"Mother, it won't go in vain. He shall be called 'Ekdant' (one-toothed)," Parashurama answered, comforting Ganesha. Shiva and Parvati forgave Parashurama.

Ganesha The Elephant-Headed God

Chapter 12
Ganesha's Journey Around the World

Shiva and Parvati wanted their two sons, Ganesha and Kartikeya, to get married. They couldn't decide who should be married first. "You both are equally dear to me. We don't want to hurt either of our sons by choosing the other," Shiva said.

To settle the situation, Shiv and Parvati decided to test them.

"I want you both to travel round the world thrice and return here. Whoever returns first will be married first," Shiva announced.

Ganesha The Elephant-Headed God

As soon as Shiva said these words, Kartikeya didn't waste a single minute and immediately hopped on to his vehicle, a peacock. By the time Ganesha mounted his vehicle, the mouse, his brother had already dashed out on his journey.

"With my huge belly and my vehicle, I can't defeat my elder brother, and it would be impossible to travel that far," Ganesha waited and pondered over the task.

He then made a decision based on his wisdom and soon came up with a solution. He went where his parents were seated. He asked for their permission and circled them thrice.

Ganesha The Elephant-Headed God

"Mother, Father! I have finished circling the world. Please make arrangements for my wedding," Ganesha said.

"Ganesha, what are you doing? We had asked the two of you to travel round the world. Your brother is ahead of you," Parvati urged him.

"I believe that my parents are my universe and are very dear to me. It's mentioned in the Vedas that anything that is dear to you becomes the centre of your life, your world,"
Ganesha stated.

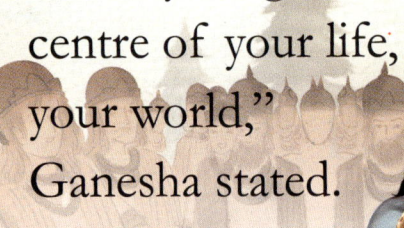

The parents were in awe of Ganesha's wit and affection. They couldn't argue with him and made arrangements for his wedding. They went to meet Vishvarua, the son of Kashyapa. Vishvarua had two daughters named Siddhi and Riddhi. Ganesha married the two sisters in a grand ceremony.

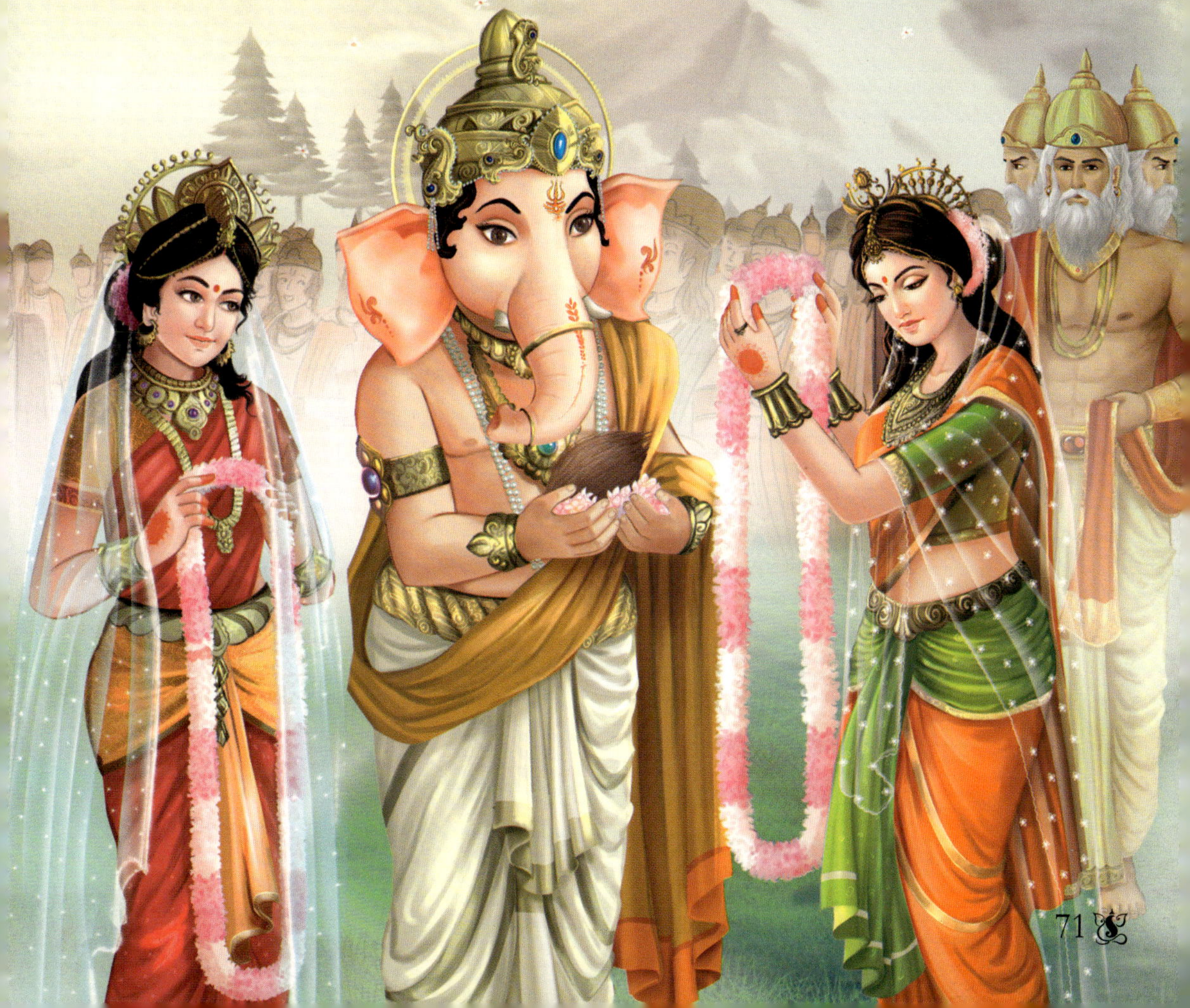

Ganesha The Elephant-Headed God

Chapter 13
The Return of Kartikeya

Many years later, Ganesha became the proud father of sons Laksha and Labha. His elder brother also returned to Mount Kailash after travelling around the world, but Kartikeya didn't expect to find Ganesha already married.

Kartikeya heard the whole story from Narad Muni. He felt cheated and decided to live separately from his family.
So, he went to Mount Krauncha and continued residing there. He never got married, and that is why he is referred to as Kumara.
Shiva and Parvati visited their elder son regularly. On the day of the new moon (Amavasya), Lord Shiva visited him, while Parvati visited him on the day of the full moon (Purnima).

Ganesha The Elephant-Headed God

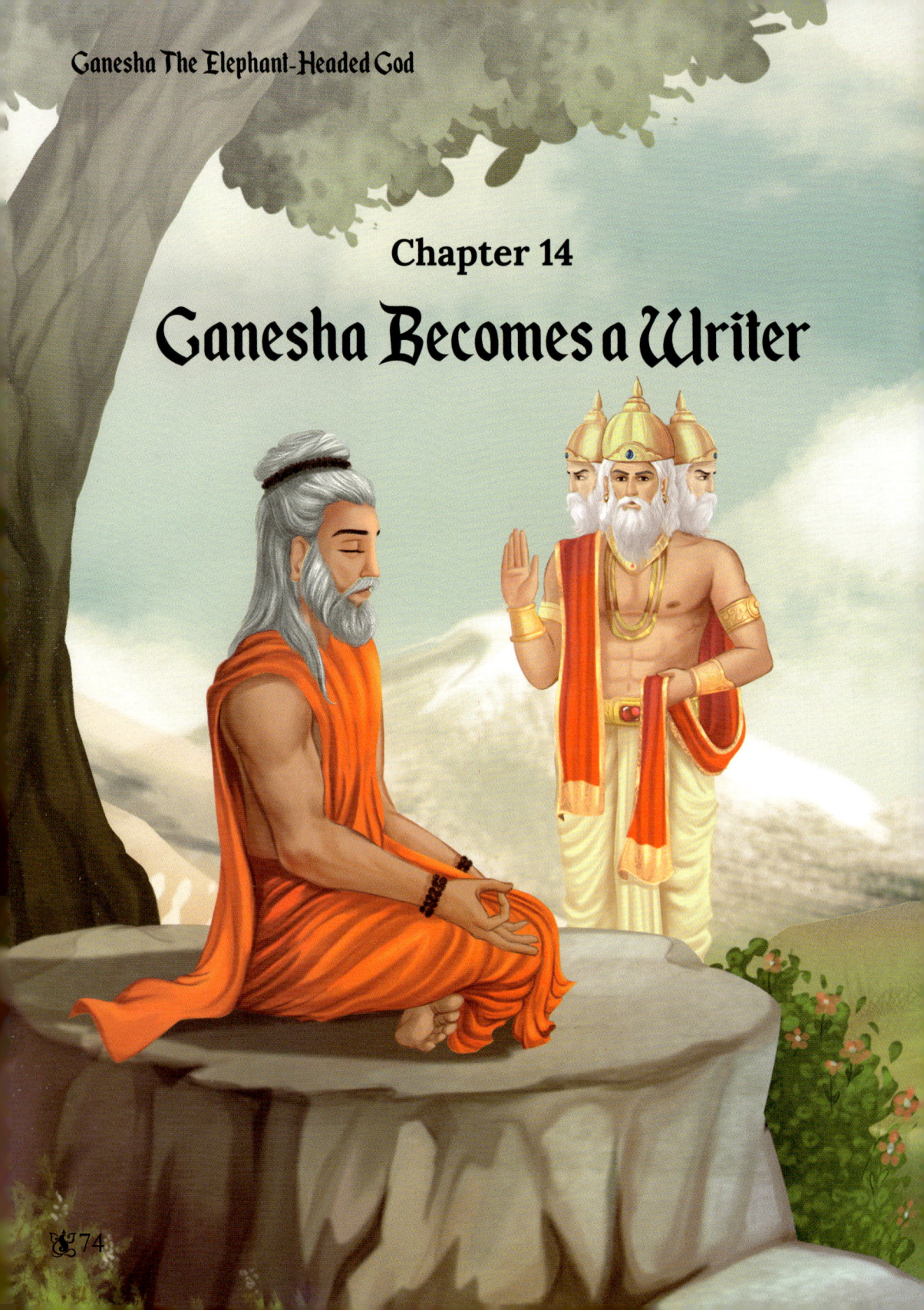

Chapter 14
Ganesha Becomes a Writer

Sage Ved Vyasa, the grandfather of the Pandavas, was once meditating in the Himalayas. Suddenly, the god of creation, Lord Brahma appeared before him and said, "As you have seen the entire story of Mahabharata, could you write it down? I think you would be the best person for this task."

Ved Vyasa knew that the Mahabharata was a very complex story and said, "Lord, I can't compose and write such a lengthy story at the same time. Please advise to me somebody who can help me write it." Brahma recommended Lord Ganesha for the task.

Ganesha The Elephant-Headed God

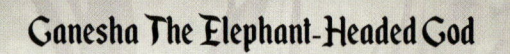

Sage Vyasa started meditating on Lord Ganesha, and soon he appeared before him. Vyasa narrated his concerns to him and requested Ganesha to become his scribe.

"I shall assist you in this task, Sage Vyasa, but on the condition that you will recite the Mahabharata non-stop," Ganesha said.

Vyasa smiled and asked Lord Ganesha for a favour, "But Ganesha, promise me that you will write only once you understand the lines that I dictate." Lord Ganesha accepted the condition.

Ganesha The Elephant-Headed God

Sage Vyasa and Ganesha began writing. Sometimes Ganesha took time to understand the complex lines narrated by Sage Vyasa. It took both of them three years of continuous speaking and writing to complete the epic.

Ganesha went back to his abode. A boon by the Devas and the Trimuti had made him immortal after the elephant head was placed on him.

The elephant-headed Ganesha, known by various names such as Ganpati and Vinayaka, is one of the most loved and revered gods in the Hindu pantheon. The son of Shiva and Parvati, he is worshipped at the beginning of all rituals and ceremonies and is also known as the remover of obstacles and the god of wisdom. He was the scribe who noted down the Mahabharata. His birthday, Ganesha Chaturthi, falls in the monsoon season and is celebrated with great pomp, festive fervour, and sweet rice dumplings called Modaks.

The End

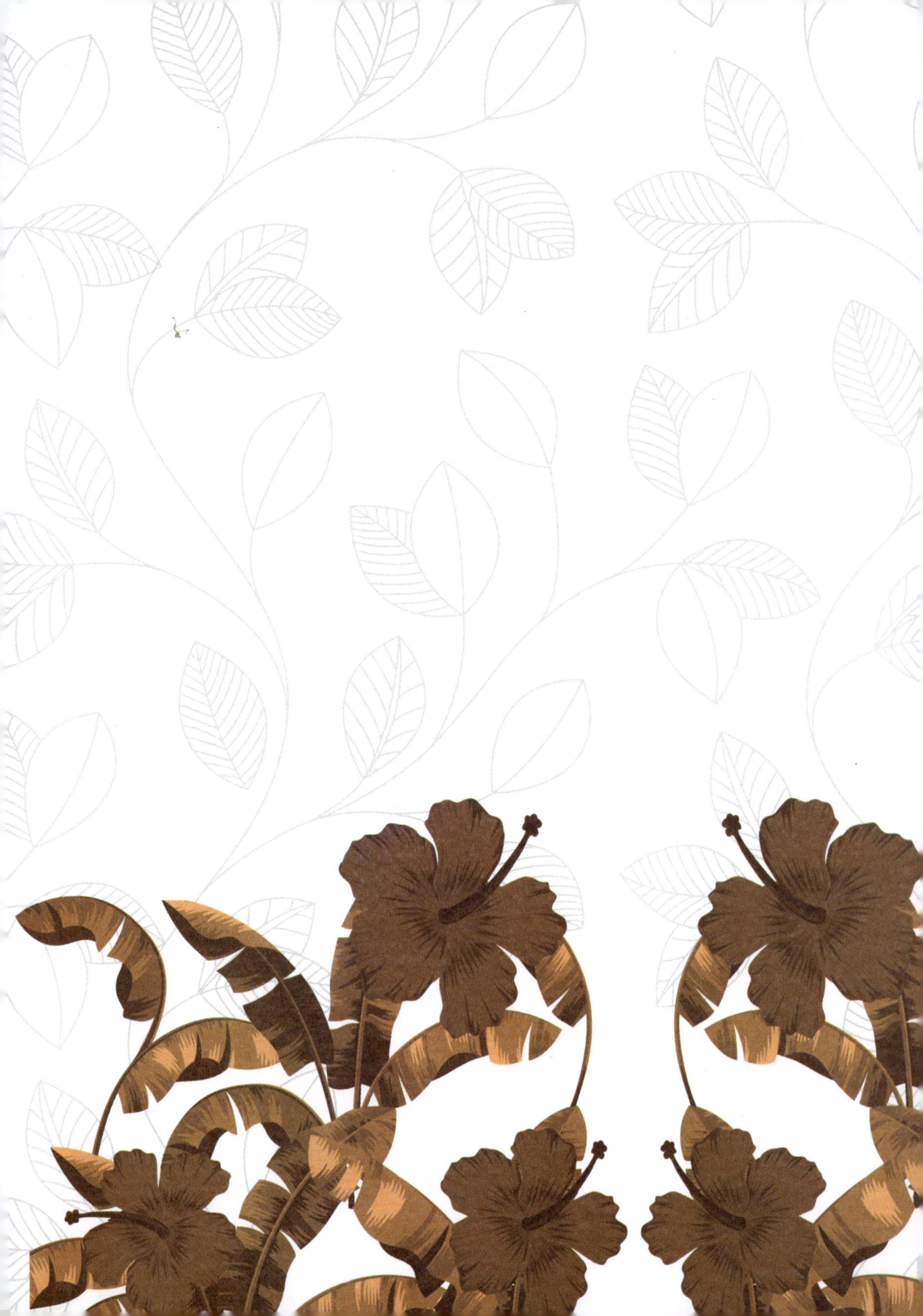